With special thanks to
Sam and his Grandad

First published 1989 by Walker Books Ltd
87 Vauxhall Walk, London SE11 5HJ

This edition published in 2008

2 4 6 8 10 9 7 5 3 1

© 1989 Blackbird Design Pty Ltd

The moral rights of the author-illustrator
have been asserted.

This book has been typeset in Times.

Printed in China

British Library Cataloguing in Publication Data:
a catalogue record for this book is
available from the British Library.

ISBN 978-1-4063-1647-6

www.walkerbooks.co.uk

Grandad's Magic

BOB GRAHAM

WALKER BOOKS
AND SUBSIDIARIES
LONDON · BOSTON · SYDNEY · AUCKLAND

Three dogs lived in Alison's house.

Two sat high on the shelf. They were very precious
to Alison's mum. They were very breakable.

Alison was not to touch them even if she could reach.
She didn't like them anyway.

Alison much preferred Rupert. He lived on the armchair.

Rupert only left the chair to have his dinner or go
to the toilet.

He wouldn't leave the chair for Alison's mum *or* her dad, and certainly not for Max, who often tried to pull his tail.

Rupert wouldn't even get out of his chair when Grandma and Grandad came to lunch on Sunday.

Alison held Max for Grandma
to kiss. He curled his fists and
kicked his legs.

"Give him to me," said Grandad.
"I know how to handle this young chap.
Now for my magic..."

Grandad reached into Max's shirt and slowly pulled out a chocolate bear. "Have you been keeping that in your shirt all this time?" he said.

Max's face lit up with pleasure.

Then Grandad lost the bear . . .

and found it again under Rupert's collar!
"It's magic," said Alison.

"Watch me, Grandad," said Alison.

She had a trick of her own. She was learning to juggle with three puffins filled with sand that Grandad had given her.

This *sounded* easy, but she had to keep them going from hand to hand. The idea was to have three puffins in the air all at once.

"Try one at a time, Alison," said Grandad. "Backwards and forwards . . .

and when you learn that, try two, and when you learn that, try three."

"I'm not as good as I used to be," said Grandad.

Sunday was the only day the china dogs came down from the shelf. Alison's mum used them as a table decoration. They guarded the fruit.

Every Sunday Grandad picked his table napkin out of the air like an apple off a tree.

And he talked of his best trick of all . . .

"I used to be able to take this tablecloth, give it a
pull in a certain kind of way, and it would whip out from
under all this stuff and leave everything standing there.

But that was a long time ago."

Then one Sunday,
Grandad noticed
how well Alison
juggled, and . . .

without warning, he removed his coat and climbed
on to the chair.

"One good trick deserves another," he said.
And he gave the tablecloth a short, snapping tug.

There was a moment of silence. Mum looked pale.
"You did it!" said Alison.
Grandad did a triumphant dance round the room.
And *that's* when it happened.

An orange rolled off the
bowl, hit one of the
precious dogs and sent it
spinning into mid-air . . .

just as Rupert happened to be making a trip to the toilet.

It settled on his very broad back...

then landed safely in Max's lap.

Alison held her breath. Would Grandad get into trouble?

But Mum smiled thinly as she put the dogs back on the shelf.
"Don't *you* try that trick, Ally," said Grandad.

The following Sunday there were a number of changes in Alison's house. When Grandma and Grandad came to lunch,

the dogs stayed on the shelf.

And the table was set with unbreakable plastic plates
and place mats.

Just before lunch, Rupert found a box of chocolates
hidden under his cushion.

Later, Grandad made the chocolates appear just like magic.
They were for Mum, who had such a shock last week.

Alison was dismayed.
"That's not magic, it's a trick!

You put them there, Grandad.
The price is still on them!"

"We performers can't get it right all the time, Alison," Grandad said, "but the chocolates have certainly vanished."

"Now, let's see how long *you* can spin this plastic plate on the end of your finger!"

BOB GRAHAM

Bob Graham is one of Australia's finest author-illustrators.
Winner of the Kate Greenaway Medal, Smarties Book Prize and CBCA
Picture Book of the Year, his stories are renowned for celebrating the magic
of everydayness. Bob says, *"I'd like reading my books to be a little like opening
a family photo album, glimpsing small moments captured from daily lives."*

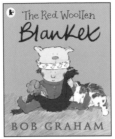

ISBN 978-1-4063-1649-0

ISBN 978-1-4063-1613-1

ISBN 978-1-4063-1647-6

ISBN 978-1-4063-1640-7

ISBN 978-1-4063-1648-3

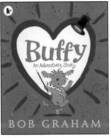

ISBN 978-1-4063-1650-6

ISBN 978-0-7445-9827-8

WINNER OF THE CBCA PICTURE BOOK
OF THE YEAR AWARD (2002)

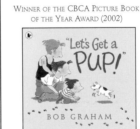

ISBN 978-1-4063-0851-8

WINNER OF THE
KATE GREENAWAY MEDAL (2002)

ISBN 978-1-84428-482-5

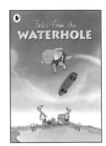

ISBN 978-1-4063-0132-8

ISBN 978-1-4063-0686-6

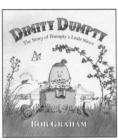

ISBN 978-1-84428-067-4

ISBN 978-1-4063-0338-4

ISBN 978-1-4063-0716-0

ISBN 978-1-4063-1492-2

Available from all good bookstores

www.walkerbooks.co.uk
www.walkerbooks.com.au